The
Never-Ending
Wrong

Books by Katherine Anne Porter

FLOWERING JUDAS

KATHERINE ANNE PORTER'S FRENCH SONG BOOK

PALE HORSE, PALE RIDER

THE LEANING TOWER

THE DAYS BEFORE

SHIP OF FOOLS

COLLECTED ESSAYS AND OCCASIONAL WRITINGS

COLLECTED STORIES OF KATHERINE ANNE PORTER

THE NEVER-ENDING WRONG

Katherine Anne Porter

The Never-Ending Wrong

An Atlantic Monthly Press Book
Little, Brown and Company · Boston · Toronto
1977

FIRST EDITION

Second Printing

This book appeared in its entirety in *The Atlantic*.

Library of Congress Cataloging in Publication Data
Porter, Katherine Anne, 1894–
  The never-ending wrong.
  "An Atlantic Monthly Press book,"
  Bibliography: p.
  1. Radicalism—United States—Case studies.
2. Sacco-Vanzetti case. 3. Porter, Katherine Anne,
1894–   I. Title.
HX86.P66   364.1   77–9393
ISBN 0–316–71391–0

ATLANTIC–LITTLE, BROWN BOOKS
ARE PUBLISHED BY
LITTLE, BROWN AND COMPANY
IN ASSOCIATION WITH
THE ATLANTIC MONTHLY PRESS

Published simultaneously in Canada
by Little, Brown & Company (Canada) Limited

PRINTED IN THE UNITED STATES OF AMERICA

This Book Is For
Lieutenant Commander William R. Wilkins

Foreword

THIS book is not for the popular or best-selling list for a few weeks or months. It is a plain, full record of a crime that belongs to history.

When a reporter from a newspaper here in Maryland asked to talk to me, he said he had heard that I was writing another book . . . what about? . . . I gave him the title and the names of Sacco and Vanzetti. There was a wavering pause . . . then: "Well, I don't really know anything about them . . . for me it's just history."

It is my conviction that when events are forgotten, buried in the cellar of the page — they are no longer even history.

List of Illustrations

The
Never-Ending
Wrong

For several years in the early 1920s when I was living part of the time in Mexico, on each return to New York, I would follow again the strange history of the Italian emigrants Nicola Sacco a shoemaker, and Bartolomeo Vanzetti a fishmonger, who were accused of a most brutal holdup of payroll guards, with murder, in South Braintree, Massachusetts, in the early afternoon of April 15, 1920. They were tried before a Massachusetts court and condemned to death almost seven years later.

In appearance it was a commonplace crime by quite ordinary, average, awkward gangsters, the only unusual feature being that these men were tried, convicted, and put to death; for gangsters in those days, at any rate those who operated boldly enough on a large scale, while not so powerful or so securely entrenched as the Mafia today, enjoyed a curious immunity in society and under the law. We have only to remember the completely public career of Al Capone, who, as chief of the bloodiest gang ever known until that time in this country, lived as if a magic circle had been drawn around him: he could at last be convicted only of not paying his income tax — that "income" he had got by methodical wholesale crime, murder, drug traffic, bootleg liquor, prostitution, and a preposterous mode of blackmail called "protection," a cash payment on demand instead of a gunpoint visit, the vampire bat of small businesses such as family delicatessens, Chinese laundries, et cetera. After serving his time on Alcatraz, he retired to Florida to live in peace and respectable luxury while his syphilitic brain softened into imbecility. When he died, there was a three-day sentimental wallow on the radio, a hysterical orgy of nostalgia for the good old times when a guy could really get away with it. I remember the tone of drooling bathos in which one of them said, "Ah, just the same, in spite of all, he was a great guy. They just don't make 'em like that anymore." Of course, time has proved since how wrong the announcer was — it is obvious they do make 'em like that nearly every day . . . like that but even more indescribably monstrous — and world radio told us day by day that this was not just local stuff, it was pandemic.

THAT of course was in a time later than this episode, this case of Sacco and Vanzetti which began so obscurely and ended as one of the important turning points in the history of this country; not the cause, but the symptom of a change so deep and so sinister in the whole point of view and direction of this people as a nation that I for one am not competent to analyze it. I only know what happened by what has happened to us since, by remembering what we were, or what many of us believed we were, before. We were most certainly then of a different cast of mind and feeling than we are now, or such a thing as the Sacco–Vanzetti protest could never have been brought about by any means; and I much doubt such a commotion could be roused again for any merciful cause at all among us.

Four incidents a good many years apart are somehow sharply related in my mind. Long ago a British judge was quoted as saying he refused clemency at popular demand to uphold the principle of capital punishment and to prove he was not to be intimidated by public protest. During Hitler's time, Himmler remarked that for the good of the state, popular complaints should be ignored, and if they persisted, the complainers should be punished. Judge Webster Thayer, during the Sacco–Vanzetti episode, was heard to boast while playing golf, "Did you see what I did to those anarchistic bastards?" and the grim little person named Rosa Baron (she shall come later) who was head of my particular group during the Sacco–Vanzetti demonstrations in Boston snapped at me when I expressed the wish that we might save the lives of Sacco and Vanzetti: "Alive

— what for? They are no earthly good to us alive."
These painful incidents illustrate at least four common perils in the legal handling that anyone faces when accused of a capital crime of which he is not guilty, especially if he has a dubious place in society, an unpopular nationality, erroneous political beliefs, the wrong religion socially, poverty, low social standing — the list could go on but this is enough. Both of these unfortunate men, Sacco and Vanzetti, suffered nearly all of these disadvantages. A fearful word had been used to cover the whole list of prejudices and misinformation, and in some deeply mysterious way, their names had been associated with it — Anarchy.

If there really was a South Braintree gang as it is claimed, to which two Anarchists belonged, it seems to have been a small affair operating under rather clumsy leadership; its real crime seems not to have been exactly robbery and murder, but political heresy: they were Anarchists it was said who robbed and murdered to get funds for their organization — in this case, Anarchy — another variation on the Robin Hood myth.

Anarchy had been a word of fear in many countries for a long time, nowhere more so than in this one; nothing in that time, not even the word "Communism," struck such terror, anger, and hatred into the popular mind; and nobody seemed to understand exactly what Anarchy as a political idea meant any more than they understood Communism, which has muddied the water to the point that it sometimes calls itself Socialism, at other times Democracy, or even in its present condition, the Republic. Fascism, Nazism, new names for very ancient evil forms of government — tyranny and dictatorship — came into fashion almost at the same time with Communism; at least the aims of those two were clear enough; at least their leaders made no attempt to deceive anyone as to their intentions. But Anarchy had been here all the nineteenth century, with its sinister offspring Nihilism, and it is a simple truth that the human mind can face better the most oppressive government, the most rigid restrictions, than the awful prospect of a lawless, frontierless world. Freedom is a dangerous intoxicant and very few people can tolerate it in any quantity; it brings out the old raiding, oppressing, murderous instincts; the rage for revenge, for power, the lust for bloodshed. The longing for freedom takes the form of crushing the enemy — there is always the enemy! — into the earth; and where and who is the enemy if there is no visible establishment to attack, to destroy with blood and fire? Remember all that oratory when freedom is threatened again. Freedom, remember, is not the same as liberty.

ON May 15, 1927, Nicola Sacco wrote from the prison in Charlestown, where he had been in and out of the death cell since July 1921, to his faithful friend Leon Henderson: "I frankly tell you, dear friend, that if he [Governor Fuller of Massachusetts] have a chance he'll hang us, and it is too bad to see you and all the other good friends this optimism while today we are facing the electric chair."

Bartolomeo Vanzetti, his fellow prisoner, wrote as early as 1924, after four years in prison convicted but not yet sentenced: "I am tired, tired, tired: I ask if to live like now, for love of life, is not rather than wisdom or heroism mere cowardness." He did consent to live on: he wished so dearly to live that he let his life be taken from him rather than take it himself. Yet near the end, he arrived apparently without help at a profound, painful understanding: "When one has reason to despair and he despairs not, he may be more abnormal than if he would despair."

They were put to death in the electric chair at Charlestown Prison at midnight on the 23rd of August, 1927, a desolate dark midnight, a night for perpetual remembrance and mourning. I was one of the many hundreds who stood in anxious vigil watching the light in the prison tower, which we had been told would fail at the moment of death; it was a moment of strange heartbreak.

THE trial of Jesus of Nazareth, the trial and rehabilitation of Joan of Arc, any one of the witchcraft trials in Salem during 1691, the Moscow trials of 1937 during which Stalin destroyed all of the founders of the 1924 Soviet Revolution, the Sacco–Vanzetti trial of 1920 through 1927 — there are many trials such as these in which the victim was already condemned to death before the trial took place, and it *took* place only to cover up the real meaning: the accused was to be put to death. These are trials in which the judge, the counsel, the jury, and the witnesses are the criminals, not the accused. For any believer in capital punishment, the fear of an honest mistake on the part of all concerned is cited as the main argument against the final terrible decision to carry out the death sentence. There is the frightful possibility in all such trials as these that the judgment has already been pronounced and the trial is just a mask for murder.

BOTH of them knew English very well — not so much in grammar and syntax but for the music, the true meaning of the words they used. They were Italian peasants, emigrants, laborers, self-educated men with an exalted sense of language as an incantation. *Read those letters!* They also had in common a distrust in general of the powers of this world, well founded in their knowledge of life as it is lived by people who work with their hands in humble trades for wages. Vanzetti had raised himself to the precarious independence of fish peddler, Sacco had learned the skilled trade of shoemaker; his small son was named Dante, and a last letter to this child is full of high-minded hopes and good counsel. At the very door of death, Sacco turned back to recall a glimpse of his wife's beauty and their happiness together. Their minds, each one in its very different way, were ragbags of faded Anarchic doctrine, of "class consciousness," of "proletarian snobbism," yet their warmth of feeling gave breath and fresh meaning to such words as Sacco wrote to Mrs. Leon Henderson: "Pardon me, Mrs. Henderson, it is not to discredit and ignore you, Mrs. Evans and other generosity work, which I sincerely believe is a noble one and I am respectful: But it is the warm sincere voice of an unrest heart and a free soul that lived and loved among the workers class all his life."

This was a state of mind, or point of view, which many of the anxious friends from another class of society found very hard to deal with, not to be met on their own bright, generous terms in this crisis of life and death; to be saying, in effect, we are all brothers and equal citizens; to receive, in effect, the reserved answer: No, not yet. It is clear now that the condemned men understood and realized their predicament much better than any individual working with any organization devoted to their rescue. Their friends from a more fortunate destiny had confidence in their own power to get what they asked of their society, their government; courts were not sacrosanct, they could be mistaken; it was a civic duty now and then to protest their judgments, persuade them by one means or another to reverse their sentences. The two laboring men, who had managed to survive and scramble up a few steps from nearly the bottom level of life, knew well from the beginning that they had every reason to despair, they did not really trust these strangers from the upper world who furnished the judges and lawyers to the courts, the politicians to the offices, the faculties to the universities, who had all the money and the influence — why should they be turning against their own class to befriend two laborers? Sacco wrote to Gardner Jackson, member of an upper-middle-class family, rich enough and ardent enough to devote his means and his time to the Sacco–Vanzetti Defense Committee: "Although we are one heart, unfortunately we represent two opposite class." What they may not have known — we can only hope they did not know — was that some of the groups apparently working for them, people of their own class in many cases, were using the occasion for Communist propaganda, and hoping only for their deaths as a political argument. I know this because I heard and saw. By chance and nothing else I was with a committee from the Communist line of defense. The exact title is of no importance. It was a mere splinter group from the national and world organization. It was quiet, discreet, at times the action seemed to be moving rather in circles; most of the volunteers, for we were all that, were no more Communists than I was. A young man who did a lot of running about, on what errands I never tried to discover, expressed what most of us thought when we learned that we were working under Communist direction: "Well, what of it? If he's fighting on my side, I'll go with the Devil!"[1]

It was the popular way of talking and a point of view fatal to any moral force or any clear view of issues; it was only a kind of catchphrase, but a symptom of the confusion of the times, the loss and denial of standards, the scumbling of boundary lines, and the whole evil trend toward reducing everything human to the mud of the lowest common demoninator.

A CERTAIN hotel near the Boston Common had been quite taken over by several separate and often rather hostile organizers of the demonstrations and I was prepared to fall eagerly and with a light heart into the atmosphere I found established there — even though it held a menace I could not instantly define — of monastic discipline, obedience, the community spirit, everybody working toward a common end, with faith in their cause and in each other. In this

---

[1] I heard this again years later from Germans in Berlin when Hitler was beginning to infect the local mind like a medieval plague.

last, I was somewhat mistaken, as I was very soon to find out. The air was stiff with the cold, mindless, irrational compliance with orders from "higher up." The whole atmosphere was rank with intrigue and deceit and the chilling realization that any one of them would have sold another to please superiors and to move himself up the ladder.

Politically I was mistaken in my hopes, also. For I see now that they were only that, based on early training in ethics and government, courses which I have not seen lately in any curriculum. Based on these teachings, I never believed that this country would alienate China in the Boxer Rebellion of 1900; or that we would not help France chase Hitler off the left bank of the Rhine, as Mussolini had chased him single-handedly out of the South Tyrol (and Mussolini himself was receiving heavy financial and political support from very powerful people in this country); or that we would let the Communists dupe us into deserting Republican Spain; or that we would abet Franco; or let Czechoslovakia, a republic we had helped to found, fall to Soviet Russia. It is quite obvious now that my political thinking was the lamentable "political illiteracy" of a liberal idealist — we might say, a species of Jeffersonian.

In the reckless phrase of the confirmed joiner in the fight for whatever relief oppressed humanity was fighting for, I had volunteered "to be useful wherever and however I could best serve," and was drafted into a Communist outfit all unknowing; this is no doubt because my name was on the list of contributors to funds in aid of Sacco and Vanzetti for several years. Even from Mexico, I sent what bits of money I could, when I could, to whatever group solicited at the moment: I never inquired as to the shades of political belief because that was not what was important to me in that cause, which concerned common humanity. In the same way, I went with the first organization that invited me, and at the Boston boat at the foot of Christopher Street was pleasantly surprised to see several quite good friends there, none of whom had any more definite political opinions than I had. I was then, as now, a registered voting member of the Democratic Party, a convinced liberal — not then a word of contempt — and a sympathizer with the new (to me) doctrines brought out of Russia from 1919 to 1920 onward by enthusiastic, sentimental, misguided men and women who were looking for a New Religion of Humanity, as one of them expressed it, and were carrying the gospel that the New Jerusalem could be expected to rise any minute in Moscow or thereabouts.

It is hard to explain, harder no doubt for a new generation to understand, how the "intellectuals" and "artists" in our country leaped with such abandoned, fanatic credulity into the Russian hell-on-earth of 1920. They quoted the stale catchphrases and slogans. They were lifted to starry patriotism by the fraudulent Communist organization called the Lincoln Brigade. The holy name was a charm which insured safety and victory. The bullet struck your Bible instead of your heart. Not all of them merit being enclosed in the pejorative quotation marks; they were quite simply the most conventionally brought-up, middle-class people of no intellectual or other pretensions. There was a Bessie Beatty who was all for the Revolution, capital "R," but who meanwhile did nicely in New York as editor of a popular magazine for women; Albert Rhys Williams, a minister's son, very religious himself, whose main recognition was based on the amusing story of how he had spent the first three days of the fall of the Russian Empire in complete formal attire — white tie, wing collar, tails — and was somewhat the worse for wear when the third day appeared. (Nobody ever explained to me how anyone, no matter how sympathetic, could have survived a true Communist revolt in that dress belonging to the most criminal of the classes of society, or how Mr. Williams, a dedicated fellow traveler, should have had occasion to appear in that outfit.) But let us go on. There was Frank Tannenbaum, Jewish by birth, a good journalist, really trying to help build a New Jerusalem anywhere and everywhere and believing firmly that the foundation stone had at last been laid in Moscow.

"For me and others like me, the Kremlin meant

the Third International, and this meant the organization of the 'workers of the world' to vindicate their human rights against everything we hated in contemporary society."[2] Edmund Wilson wrote that, as well and clearly expressed as it has been until now.

"I have seen the future and it works." Lincoln Steffens is reported to have said this, though it has been much denied. It is claimed that he did not ever say such a reckless thing. He was there, on the spot, admiring everything in Russia at the time of William Bullitt's 1919 visit to Russia, carrying on a delightful social life, although no one says quite how it was done in that particular atmosphere. I can say, once for all, that he may not have said this in Russia, but I heard him say it in Mexico in 1922 at a victorious desert celebration where the President, the Cabinet, "Congress," and all the radical politicians in the government were holding a great fiesta on a wonderful hot dusty day, where there were dozens of mariachi bands playing — drums and trumpets going — and all of us were sitting on the ground in a joyous picnic spirit eating *mole*, the national dish. I was with a party with which Mr. Steffens had come to see what a true revolution could do for people who needed a revolution. He was frightfully unhappy and uncomfortable. He did not like sitting on the ground and he did not see the beauty and the picturesque-

---

[2] Edmund Wilson, *The American Earthquake,* page 573, chapter called "Postscript of 1957."

ness of the Indians' figures and clothing, and he referred to them as "uncivilized." He could not endure the sight, the taste, the smell, or even the presence of the *mole;* it was very peppery. The rest of the party were eating and scraping up the sauce with savory folded tortillas. His eyes behind their thick glasses swiveled around once at us and he said, "I wish you could see your mouths — you would rub your faces in the sand to clean them up."

It was some time later that afternoon when we were discussing world events, and all of us wanted to know how in the world Russian people could survive the latest disaster to their government, and he said: "All progress takes its toll in human life. Russia is the coming power of the world. I have seen the future and it works." So much for that. No matter how sad it may seem now, Mr. Steffens said it then, jovially, but in earnest. I wrote it down word for word, then and there, in my notebook.

M Y group was headed by Rosa Baron, a dry, fanatical little woman who wore thick-lensed spectacles over her blue, accusing eyes — a born whip hand, who talked an almost impenetrable jargon of party dogma. Her "approach" to every "question" (and everything *was* a question) was "purely dialectical." Phrases such as "capitalistic imperialism," "bourgeois morality," "slave mentality," "the dictatorship of the proletariat," "the historical imperative" (meaning more or less, I gathered, that history makes man and not the other way around), "the triumph of the workers," "social consciousness," and "political illiteracy" flew from her dry lips all day long. She viewed a "political illiterate" as a conventional mind might a person of those long-ago days born out of wedlock: an unfortunate condition, but reprehensible and without remedy even for its victim. Conservative was only a slightly less pejorative term than Reactionary, and as for Liberal, it was a dirty word, quite often linked in speech with other vaguely descriptive words, even dirtier, if possible. There were many such groups, for this demonstration had been agitated for and prepared for many years by the Communists. They had not originated the protest, I believe, but had joined in and tried to take over, as their policy was, and is. Their presence created the same confusion, beclouding the issue and discrediting the cause as it always had done and as they intended it to do. It appeared in its true form and on its most disastrous scale in Spain later. They were well organized to promote disorder and to prevent any question ever being settled — but I had not then discovered this; I remarked to our Communist leader that even then, at that late time, I still hoped the lives of Sacco and Vanzetti might be saved and that they would be granted another trial. "Saved," she said, ringing a change on her favorite answer to political illiteracy, "who wants them saved? What earthly good would they do us alive?"

I was another of those bourgeois liberals who got in the way of serious business, yet we were needed, by the thousands if possible, for this great agitation must be made to appear to be a spontaneous uprising of the American people, and for practical reasons, the more non-Communists, the better. They were all sentimental bleeders, easily impressed.

Rosa Baron's young brother once presumed to argue with her on some point of doctrine when I was present. "I'll report you to the Committee," she said, "if you talk about Party business before outsiders." This was the first time I had ever come face to face, here and now personally, with the Inquisitorial spirit hard at work.

"FROM each according to his capacity, to each according to his need."

Lenin was known to think little of people who let their human feelings for decency get in the way of the revolution which was to save mankind; he spoke contemptuously of the "saints" who kept getting underfoot; he had only harsh words for those "weak sisters" who flew off the "locomotive of history" every time it rounded a sharp curve. History was whatever was happening in Russia, and the weak sisters, who sometimes called themselves "fellow travelers," were perhaps, many of them, jolted by the collision with what appeared to be a dream of the ideal society come true, dazzled by the bright colors of a false dawn.

I flew off Lenin's locomotive and his vision of history in a wide arc in Boston, Massachusetts, on August 21, 1927; it was two days before the putting to death of Sacco and Vanzetti, to the great ideological satisfaction of the Communist-headed group with which I had gone up to Boston. It was exactly what they had hoped for and predicted from the first: another injustice of the iniquitous capitalistic system against the working class.

Toasts were drunk at parties "To the Red Dawn" — a very pretty image indeed. "See you on the barricades!" friends would say at the end of an evening of dancing in Harlem. Nobody thought any of this strange; in those days the confusion on this subject by true believers, though not great, was not quite so bad and certainly not so sinister as it is now. It was not then subversive to associate with Communists, nor even treasonable to belong to the Communist Party. It is true that Communists, or a lot of people who thought themselves Communists — and it is astonishing how many of them have right-about-faced since they got a look at the real thing in action — held loud meetings in Union Square, and they often managed to get a few heads cracked by the police —

all the better! Just the proof they needed of the brutalities of the American Gestapo. On the other hand, they could gather thousands of "sympathizers" of every shade of political and religious belief and every known nationality and carry off great May Day parades peaceably under police protection. The innocent fellow travelers of this country were kept in a state of excited philanthropy by carefully planted stories of the struggle that the great Russian reformers were having against local rebellious peasants, blasted crops, and plagues of various kinds, bringing the government almost to starvation. Our fellow travelers picketed, rebuking our government for failure to send food and other necessaries to aid the great cause in that courageous country. I do not dare say that our government responded to these childish appeals, but tons upon tons of good winter wheat and other supplies were sent in fabulous quantities. It turned out that the threatened famine took place there — it was real — under orders from Lenin, who directed a great famine or an occasional massacre by way of bringing dissidence under the yoke, and I remember one blood-curdling sentence from a letter of his to a subordinate, directing him to conduct a certain massacre as "a model of mercilessness."

What struck me later was that I had already met and talked to refugees from Russia in Mexico who had got out with their lives and never ceased to be amazed at it. In New York I saw picketing in Times Square and Wall Street, solemn placard-carrying processions of second-generation descendants of those desolate, ragged, hopeful people who had landed on Ellis Island from almost every country in the West, escaping from the dreadful fates now being suffered by their blood kin in Russia and other parts of the world. Not one of them apparently could see that the starvation and disease and utter misery were brought on methodically and most successfully for the best of political and economic reasons without any help from us, while the Party was being fed richly with our wheat.

Then there was AMTORG, headquartered in New York, managed by a Russian Jewish businessman of the cold steel variety, advertised as a perfectly legal business organization for honest, aboveboard trade with the Soviets.

There was ROSTA (later TASS), the official Russian news agency and propaganda center in America, run by an American citizen, Kenneth Durant, who enjoyed perfect immunity in every Red scare of the period when dozens of suspects were arrested — not he. I assisted the editor of ROSTA for a short time and I know the subsidy was small, although the agency was accused of enjoying floods of "Moscow gold." If this was so, I don't know where it went. The editor claimed that Moscow gold was passed out at the rate of $75.00 a week for salaries (he took

$50.00 and gave me $25.00). A perennial candidate for President of the United States popped up every four years regularly on the Communist ticket — an honest man. I knew nothing of his private politics, but his public life was admirable and his doctrine was pure Christian theory.

ONCE on the picket line, I took a good look at the crowd moving slowly forward. I wouldn't have expected to see some of them on the same street, much less the same picket line and in the same jail. I knew very few people in that first picket line, but I remember Lola Ridge, John Dos Passos, Paxton Hibben, Michael Gold, Helen O'Lochlain Crowe, James Rorty, Edna St. Vincent Millay, Willie Gropper, Grace Lumpkin, all very well known then and mostly favorably — most of them have vanished, and I wonder who but me is alive to remember them now? I have a strangely tender memory of them all, as well as the faces of strangers who were being led away by the police.

We were as miscellaneous, improbable, almost entirely unassorted a gathering of people to one place in one cause as ever happened in this country. I say almost because among the pickets I did not see anyone identifiably a workingman, or "proletarian," as our Marxist "dialecticians" insisted on calling everybody who worked for his living in a factory, or as they said, "sweatshop," or "slave mill," or "salt mine." It is true that these were workdays and maybe all the workingmen were at their jobs. Suppose one of them said to his boss, "I want a day off, with pay, to picket for Sacco and Vanzetti." He would be free to picket at his leisure from then on, no doubt. There were plenty of people of the working class there, but they had risen in the world and had become professional paid proletarians, recruits to the intelligentsia, dabbling in ideas as editors, lawyers, agitators, writers who dressed and behaved and looked quite a lot like the bourgeoisie they were out to annihilate. What a vocabulary — proletarian, intelligentsia, bourgeoisie, dialectic — pure exotics transplanted from the never-never-land of the theoretically classless society which could not take root and finally withered on the stalk. Yet, they had three classes of their own and were drawing the lines shrewdly. During that time I went to a meeting of radicals of all kinds and shades, most of them workers, but not all by any means; and Michael Gold made a speech and kept repeating: "Stick to your class, *damn it, stick* to your *class*." It struck me as being such good advice that I decided to take it and tiptoed out the way one leaves church before the end.

Each morning I left the hotel, walked into the blazing August sun, and dropped into the picket line before the State House; the police would allow us to march around once or twice, then close in and make the arrests we invited; indeed, what else were we there for? My elbow was always taken quietly by the same mild little blond officer, day after day; he was very Irish, very patient, very damned bored with the whole incomprehensible show. We always greeted each other politely. It was generally understood that the Pink Tea Squad, white cotton gloves and all, had been assigned to this job, well instructed that in no circumstance were they to forget themselves and whack a lady with their truncheons, no matter how far she forgot herself in rudeness and contrariety. In fact, I never saw a lady — or a gentleman either — being rude to a policeman in that picket line, nor any act of rudeness from a single policeman. That sort of thing was to come later, from officers on different duty. The first time I was arrested, my policeman and I walked along stealing perplexed, questioning glances at each other; the gulf between us was fixed, but not impassable; neither of us wished to deny that the other was a human being; there was no natural hostility between us. I had been brought up in the fixed social belief that the whole police system existed to protect and befriend me and all my kind. Without giving this theory any attention, I had found no reason to doubt it.

Here are some notes of my conversations with my policeman during our several journeys under the

August sun, down the rocky road to the Joy Street Station:

He: "What good do you think you're doing?"

I: "I hope a *little* . . . I don't believe they had a fair trial. That is all I want for them, a fair trial."

He: "This is no way to go about getting it. You ought to know you'll *never* get anywhere with this stuff."

I: "Why not?"

He: "It makes people mad. They take you for a lot of tramps."

I: "We did everything else we could think of first, for years and years, and nothing worked."

He: "I don't believe in showing contempt for the courts this way."

I: "Neither do I, in principle. But this time the court is wrong."

He: "I trust the courts of the land more than I do all these sapheads making public riot."

I: "We aren't rioting. Look at us, how calm we are."

He (still mildly): "What I think is, you all ought to be put in jail and kept there till it's over."

I: "They don't want us in jail. There isn't enough room there."

Second day:

He (taking my elbow and drawing me out of the line; I go like a lamb): "Well, what have you been doing since yesterday?"

I: "Mostly copying Sacco's and Vanzetti's letters. I

wish you could read them. You'd believe in them if you could read the letters."

He: "Well, I don't have much time for reading."

Third day:

The picket line was crowded, anxious, and slow-moving. I reached the rounding point before I saw my policeman taking his place. I moved out and reached for his arm before we spoke. "You're late," I said, not in the least meaning to be funny. He astonished me by nearly smiling. "What have we got to hurry for?" he inquired, and my scalp shuddered — we moved on in silence.

This was the 23rd of August, the day set for the execution, and the crowds of onlookers that had gathered every morning were becoming rather noisy and abusive. My officer and I ran into a light shower of stones, a sprinkling of flowers, confetti, and a flurry of boos, catcalls, and cheers as we rounded the corner into Joy Street. We ducked our heads and I looked back and saw other prisoners and other policemen put up their hands and turn away their faces.

I: "Can you make out which is for which of us? I can't."

He: "No, I can't, and I don't care."

Silence.

He: "How many times have you been down this street today?"

I: "Only once. I was only sent out once today. How many times for you?"

It was now late afternoon, and as it turned out, this was the last picket line to form. The battle was lost and all of us knew it by then.

He (in mortal weariness): "God alone knows."

As we stood waiting in line at the desk, I said, "I expect this will be the last time you'll have to arrest me. You've been very kind and patient and I thank you."

I remember the blinded exhaustion of his face, its gray pallor with greenish shadows in it. He said "Thank *you*," and stood beside me at the desk while my name was written into the record once more. We did not speak or look at each other again, but as I followed the matron to a cell I saw him working his way slowly outward through the crowd.

The same plain, middle-aged, rather officious woman with a gold front tooth always came and put me in a cell and locked the door. Sometimes I was alone in the foggy light and stale air, being forbidden to smoke and wishing for something to read. Sometimes there would be other women, though never once a soul I knew, and we would begin at once to talk, to exchange our gossip and rumors and ideas, for, being in the dead center of this disturbance, it was quite hard to find out what was really happening. After a time, usually two or three hours, the matron would come with her keys, open the door, and say, "Come on out." Out we would come, knowing that Mr. Edward James, Henry James's nephew, was there again, putting up our bail, getting us set free for the next round. Helen O'Lochlain Crowe, who had trained with Jim Larkin as his disciple and mistress in the Irish Trouble, tried to refuse bail, insisted on staying in prison, and was finally hauled out and set on the sidewalk. Not roughly, just firmly and finally. She was, her jailers told her, bailed out whether she liked it or not, and this was very ungrateful behavior to Mr. James who was only trying to help.

Mr. James was a thin, stiff, parchment roll of a man, maybe sixty years old, immaculately turned out in tones of expensive-looking gray from head to foot, to match his gray pointed beard and his severe pale gray eyes with irritable points of light in them. He left the hall once with several of my group, and the dark young Portuguese boy who always came with him walked beside me. He was a picture of exuberance, with his oily, swarthy skin, his thick, glistening black hair, the soft corners of his full red mouth always a little moist; his young, lazy fat heaving and walloping at every step. I asked him what organization they were working with, for by now I knew too well that this whole protest was the work of a complicated machine or a set of machines working together, even if not always intentionally or with the same motives, and we were all of us being put rather expertly through set paces by distant operators, unknown manipulators whose motives and designs were far different from ours. "Oh, Mr. James and I," said the smiling, eupeptic being trundling along at my side, his red silk scarf necktie flapping, "we have our own little organization. I'm Mr. James's secretary," he said in his childish voice, "and we are perfectly independent!" He gave a coy little bounce and wiggle. He was as contented and unconcerned as a piglet in clover.

"That's charming," I said in a breath of relief from the distrust and fright growing in my mind as if I had breathed an infection from the air, "it's nice to know someone is acting on his own!"

"Mr. James and me, we've been working on this for *years!*"

I HAVE only to sort out and copy these notes down here to realize how long fifty years are, not only in the life of an individual, but of a nation, a world — to realize again, not for the first time, how one sets out for a certain goal and ends at another, different, unforeseen, and too often dismaying. We need restored to us of course that blinded obscured third eye said once to exist in the top of the brain for our guidance. Lacking it we go skew-gee in great numbers, especially those of us brought up so believingly on Judeo-Greek-Christian ethics, prone to trust the good faith of our fellows, and therefore vulnerable to betrayal because of our virtues, such as they are; that is to say, our human weaknesses. There are many notes, saved almost at random these long past years, many by mere chance; they were scrambled together in a battered yellow envelope marked Sacco–Vanzetti, and had worked their way to the bottom of many a basket of papers in many a change of houses, cities, and even a change of country. They are my personal experiences of the whirlwinds of change that brought Lenin, Stalin, Mussolini, Franco, and Hitler crowded into one half a century or less; and my understanding of this event in Boston as one of the most portentous in the long death of the civilization made by Europeans in the Western world, in the millennial upheaval which brings always every possible change but one — the two nearly matched forces of human nature, the will to give life and the will to destroy it. So, at that time and after what I have learned since, it seems strange that I was not better informed at Boston about my committee until I arrived there and was seated at a typewriter copying the Sacco and Vanzetti letters to the world. However, I was not informed and I did not ask, and this is a story of what happened, not what should have been.

AFTER more than half a long lifetime, I find that any recollection, however vivid and lasting, must unavoidably be mixed with many afterthoughts. It is hard to remember anything perfectly straight, accurate, no matter whether it was painful or pleasant at that time. I find that I remember best just what I felt and thought about this event in its own time, in its inalterable setting; my impressions of this occasion remain fast, no matter how many reviews or recollections or how many afterthoughts have added themselves with the years. It is fifty years, very long ones, since Sacco and Vanzetti were put to death in Boston, accused and convicted of a bitter crime, of which, it is still claimed, they may or may not have been guilty. I did not know then and I still do not know whether they were guilty (in spite of reading at this late day the learned, stupendous, dearly human work of attorney Herbert B. Ehrmann), but still I had my reasons for being there to protest the terrible penalty they were condemned to suffer; these reasons were of the heart, which I believe appears in these pages with emphasis. The core of this account of that fearful episode was written nearly a half-century ago, during the time in Boston and later; for years I refused to read, to talk or listen, because I couldn't endure the memory — I wanted to escape from it. Some of the account was written at the scene of the tragedy itself and, except for a word or two here and there in those early notes, where I have added a line in the hope of a clearer statement, it is unchanged in feeling and point of view. The evils prophesied by that crisis have all come true and are enormous in weight and variety.

Arrested for picketing: Edna St. Vincent Millay (left);
Lola Ridge (right).

Sacco and Vanzetti (fifth and sixth from left) on one of
their daily trips back to jail from the Dedham courthouse.

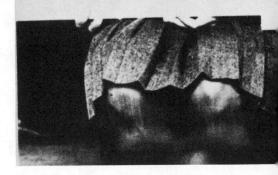

GOVERNOR FULLER!

If Your Conscience Is Clear Why

Did You Keep Investigation Secret?

(Left to right) Protesters Elizabeth Merrill (Vassar 1924), Paxton Hibben, and Katherine Anne Porter.

ey Are Not Innocent

e You Afraid of A New Trial

GOVERNOR FULLER!
Why Did You Call All Our
Witnesses Liars?

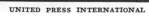

Bound for the Joy Street police station. The author (fourth from left) and "her" policeman.

Books have been written by many illustrious persons who took part in that strange event — a lawyer who was to be an Associate Justice of the Supreme Court, Felix Frankfurter, and others; a lady who was to be American Minister to Norway, Mrs. J. Borden ("Daisy") Harriman, was attending meetings there; celebrated faculty members from universities, such as Paxton Hibben; novelists such as John Dos Passos; poets such as Edna St. Vincent Millay; all of whom the public knew well, at least by name. There were many politicians in full career, some of them risking their careers by their appearances in Boston — useless to name names, there were too many, all reputable and with good influence — all of them streamed sooner or later through that large but crowded room where I sat, among other members of my special committee, at the typewriter, doing what was called "kitchen police," that is, all the dull, dusty little jobs that the more important committee members couldn't be burdened with. This was my good luck. My work was not only the melancholy pleasure of copying Sacco's and Vanzetti's letters to their friends working for them on the outside, or even of composing propaganda in the form of news items which I doubt ever got printed. I did not see a newspaper the whole time. Now and then the pioneer lady Minister, pleasant Daisy Harriman, floated in all white, horsehaired lace garden hats and pink or maybe blue chiffon frocks, on her way to or from some social afternoon festivity. She sat beside my desk one day when I had just returned from my daily picketing and said, "One needs a little recreation, even in these terrible times. You should just go out and get a little breath of fresh air — a quiet walk by yourself."

I said, "My idea of recreation would be a nice long night's sleep," for the evenings, six of them, usually were spent at some fevered mass meeting or sitting about talking with the rather random groups that formed in one stifling hot hotel room or another. I said to her, "I sometimes wonder what we are doing really. The whole thing is losing shape in my mind, but I can only hope we may learn something we need to know — that something good will come of this."

She said very gently, "What good? — Oh, they'll forget all about it. Most of them are just here for the excitement. They don't really know what is going on; and they want to forget anything unpleasant." Her broad, healthy face smiled reassuringly from under its flowering shade. Intoxicating perfume waved from her spread handkerchief when she dried her forehead. I repeated what John Dos Passos once remarked on the "imbecile" (or was the word "idiot"?) lack of memory of the human race, generally speaking.

THERE was the charming good woman of great riches and even greater charity and sweetness of mind — Mrs. Leon Henderson — who had been a champion of Sacco's and Vanzetti's from the first. I trusted her delicate, intuitional mind. She had been prodigal of all her resources, money and energy and imaginative stratagems and loving kindness. Now, at the end, when she rightly feared the worst, she was writing them letters to persuade them to break their fast, to save their strength for the new trial she was sure they would be given. She was a vegetarian and advised them to drink milk and fruit juice by way of easing themselves back into a regular diet.

She invited me to lunch. I did not then know she was a vegetarian and when she asked me what I would like, I asked for broiled lamb chops. She shuddered a little, the pupils of her eyes dilated, and she gave me a little lecture on cruelty to animals, just the same.

"I could not eat any food that had the taint of suffering and death in it; imagine my dear! Eating blood?"

I retracted at once, in painful embarrassment, and ate a savory lunch of scrambled eggs and spinach with her, and things went on very nicely. Still, I could not avoid seeing her very handsome leather handbag, her suede shoes and belt, and a light summer fur of some species I was unable to identify lying across her shoulders. My mind would wander from our topic while, bewildered once more by the confusions in human feelings, above all my own, I gazed into the glass eyes of the small, unknown, peaked-faced animal.

"We should be very wrong to despair," she said as we were getting ready to go, "even if their lives are taken away from them; nothing can take away the truth of our wish to help them, the fact of their courage in the face of death; they have never despaired or become bitter."

I said, "Yes, and if they are innocent, it must be almost unbearable not to have had the chance to prove it . . ."

She was shocked at this. "Do you mean you have a *doubt* of their innocence?" she asked.

"I simply don't know," I told her. "I thought one of the questions in this whole uproar is just precisely that — that they have not had a fair trial."

"Fair trial or not," she said — by now we were standing on the corner ready to separate — "that is not the point at all, my dear. They are innocent and their death will be a legal crime."

I have described that scene and the conversation from the notes I took when I got back to my desk at the hotel that day.

SEVERAL of the more enterprising young reporters, who were swarming over the scene like crows to a freshly planted cornfield, had put out a few invitations to some of the girls in the various groups to something they called "a little party." Rosa Baron, the head of my committee, went into action with the authority and prudence of a boarding school chaperone. "Just don't go, that's all," she told her two or three eligibles, "just don't be seen with them. That is the one thing we can't afford — a scandal of that kind!" So we didn't accept any invitations, and heard nothing more about them.

I REMEMBER small, slender Mrs. Sacco with her fine copper-colored hair and dark brown, soft, dazed eyes moving from face to face but still smiling uncertainly, surrounded in our offices by women pitying and cuddling her, sympathetic with her as if she were a pretty little girl; they spoke to her as if she were five years old or did not understand — this Italian peasant wife who, for seven long years, had shown moral stamina and emotional stability enough to furnish half a dozen women amply. I was humiliated for them, for their apparent insensibility. But I was mistaken in my anxiety — their wish to help, to show her their concern, was real, their feelings were true and lasting, no matter how awkwardly expressed; their love and tenderness and wish to help were from the heart. All through those last days in Boston, those strangely innocent women enlisted their altar societies, their card clubs, their literary round tables, their music circles, and their various charities in the campaign to save Sacco and Vanzetti. On their rounds, they came now and then to the office of my outfit in their smart thin frocks, stylish hats, and their indefinable air of eager sweetness and light, bringing money they had collected in the endless, wittily devious ways of women's organizations. They would talk among themselves and to her about how they felt, with tears in their eyes, promising to come again soon with more help. They were known as "sob sisters" by the cynics and the hangers-on of the committee I belonged to who took their money and described their activities as "sentimental orgies," of course with sexual overtones, and they jeered at "bourgeois morality." "Morality" was a word along with "charitable" and "humanitarian" and "liberal," all, at one time, in the odor of sanctity but now despoiled and rotting in the gutter where suddenly it seemed they belonged. I found myself on the side of the women; I resented the nasty things said about them by these self-appointed world reformers and I thought again, as I had more than once in Mexico, that yes, the world was a frightening enough place as it was, but think what a hell it would be if such people really got the power to do the things they planned.[3]

A LAST, huge rally took place the night before the execution, with Rosa Sacco and Luigia Vanzetti, Vanzetti's sister, on the platform. Luigia had been

---

[3] They seem to have it and are getting on with it — 1976.

brought from Italy and taken through Paris, where she had been photographed as she was marched through the streets at the head of an enormous crowd — the gaunt, striding figure of a middle-aged, plain woman who looked more like a prisoner herself than the leader of a public protest. Now they brought her forward with Mrs. Sacco and the two timid women faced the raging crowd, mostly Italians, who rose at them in savage sympathy, shouting, tears pouring down their faces, shaking their fists and calling childish phrases, their promises of revenge for their wrongs. "Never you mind, Rosina! You wait, Luigia! They'll pay, they'll pay! Don't be afraid . . . !" Rosa Sacco spread her hands over her face, but Luigia Vanzetti stared stonily down into their distorted faces with a pure horror in her own. They screamed their violence at her in her own language, trying to hearten her, but she was not consoled. She was led away like a corpse walking. The crowd roared and cursed and wept and threatened. It was the most awesome, the most bitter scene I had ever witnessed.

As we crowded out to the street, a great mass of police all around us, one of the enterprising young reporters who had helped to get up the "little party" for the girls seized my wrist, calling out, "Was this a swell show, I ask you? Did it come off like a house afire? It was all my idea; I got the whole thing up!" *His* face was savage too, wild with his triumph. "I

[39]

got Luigia out of bed to come here. She said she was too sick, but I got her up! I said, 'Don't you want to help your brother?' "

"She speaks English?" I asked in wonder at him. "What did she say?" I had rather liked him before. I have forgotten his name.

"Hell no!" he said. "She's got an interpreter. She didn't say anything; she just got up and came along."

The most terrible irony of this incident of Luigia Vanzetti I learned later: that Mussolini wrote a personal letter to Governor Fuller of Massachusetts asking for mercy for the two Italians. I had known and talked with a number of the earlier refugees from Mussolini's Italy of 1922 and onward in Mexico, and I knew well what his mercy was like toward anyone unlucky enough to displease him. But at that time, Mussolini had many admirers and defenders in this country — he was more than respectable; he was getting enormous flattering publicity. There was a group of Mussolini enthusiasts in Boston, picketing and working and going to jail and being let out, then putting their heads together in the evening to sing "Giovinezza." No harm done. The Communists thought them beneath contempt, and the liberals, the true democrats as they believed themselves to be, were then in the heyday of practicing what they preached, and were ready to fight and die for anybody's right to his own beliefs, no matter what — religious, social, or political. I thought wryly of Vol-

taire's impassioned defense of an individual's right
to say what he believed, but all I could salvage at
that time was that *I* disagreed with most of what
some of these "liberals" were saying and *I* would
defend to the death my right to disagree. "Ha," said
my little publicity inventor, listening a split second
to the sweating, howling, cheering crowd — "Talk
about free speech! How's that? Their heads will be
the first to roll." This phrase was one of the Communist crowd's favorites, and the very thought of rolling
heads would bring a mean, relishing smile to even
the dourest face.

A<small>FTER</small> Mr. James had bailed us out for the last time,
we returned to the hotel and got ready to go to the
Charlestown Prison where the execution was to take
place at midnight. It seems odd, perhaps, but I
joined with a group of persons to go in a taxi to the
prison and I cannot remember a name or a face
among them. It is possible that they were all
strangers to me. There were several hundred of us
who had been picketing in relays all day, every day
from the 21st and for four days, and their faces and
names, perhaps known at that moment, have vanished; and yet, when the thing was done, I remember
returning with persons well known to me and several
incidents which happened later. The driver of our
cab did not want us to go to the Charlestown Prison.
Neither did the police stationed at regular distances

along the whole route. They stopped our cab and turned us back half a dozen times. We would direct the driver to go a roundabout way, or to take a less traveled street. But at last, he refused to drive farther. We left him then, after making up the fare among ourselves. I was nearly penniless and I know now that a good many others among us were too. We walked on toward the prison, coming as near as we could, for the crowd was enormous and in the dim light silent, almost motionless, like crowds seen in a dream. I was never in that place but once, but I seem to remember it was a great open square with the crowd massed back from a center the police worked constantly to keep clear. They were all mounted on fine horses and loaded with pistols and hand grenades and tear gas bombs. They galloped about, bearing down upon anybody who ventured out beyond the edge of the crowd, charging and then pulling their horses up short violently so that they reared and their forehoofs beat in the air over a human head, but always swerving sharply and coming down on one side. They were trained, probably, to this spectacular, dangerous-looking performance, but still, I know it is very hard to force a good horse to step on any living thing. I have seen them in their stalls at home shudder all over at stepping on a stray, newly hatched chicken. I do not believe the police meant for the hoofs to strike and crush heads — it possibly was just a very showy technique for intimidating and controlling a mob.

This was not a mob, however. It was a silent, intent assembly of citizens — of anxious people come to bear witness and to protest against the terrible wrong about to be committed, not only against the two men about to die, but against all of us, against our common humanity and our shared will to avert what we believed to be not merely a failure in the use of the instrument of the law, an injustice committed through mere human weakness and misunderstanding, but a blindly arrogant, self-righteous determination not to be moved by any arguments, the obstinate assumption of the infallibility of a handful of men intoxicated with the vanity of power and gone mad with wounded self-importance.

A few foolish persons played a kind of game with the police, waiting until they had turned to charge in the other direction, stepping out defiantly into the center, rushing with raucous yells of glee back to safety when the police turned their horses and came on again. But these were only the lunatic fringe that follows excitement — anything will do. Most of the people moved back passively before the police, almost as if they ignored their presence; yet there were faces fixed in agonized disbelief, their eyes followed the rushing horses as if this was not a sight they had expected to see in their lives. One tall, thin figure of a woman stepped out alone, a good distance into the empty square, and when the police came down at her and the horse's hoofs beat over her head, she did not move, but stood with her shoulders slightly bowed, entirely still. The charge was repeated again and again, but she was not to be driven away. A man near me said in horror, suddenly recognizing her, "That's Lola Ridge!" and dashed into the empty space toward her. Without any words or a moment's pause, he simply seized her by the shoulders and walked her in front of him back to the edge of the crowd, where she stood as if she were half-conscious. I came near her and said, "Oh no, don't let them hurt you! They've done enough damage already." And she said, "This is the beginning of the end — we have lost something we shan't find again." I remember her bitter hot breath and her deathlike face. She had not long to live.

For an endless dreary time we had stood there, massed in a measureless darkness, waiting, watching the light in the tower of the prison. At midnight, this light winked off, winked on and off again, and my blood chills remembering it even now — I do not remember how often, but we were told that the extinction of this light corresponded to the number of charges of electricity sent through the bodies of Sacco and Vanzetti. This was not true, as the newspapers informed us in the morning. It was only one of many senseless rumors and inventions added to the smothering air. It was reported later that Sacco was harder to kill than Vanzetti — two or three shocks for that tough body. Almost at once, in small groups, the orderly, subdued people began to scatter, in a sound of voices that was deep, mournful, vast, and wavering. They walked slowly toward the center of Boston. Life felt very grubby and mean, as if we were all of us soiled and disgraced and would never in this world live it down. I said something like this to the man walking near me, whose name or face I never knew, but I remember his words — "What are you talking about?" he asked bitterly, and answered himself: "There's no such thing as disgrace any-more."

I DON'T remember where we left Lola Ridge, nor how it came about that a certain number of us gathered in one of the hotel rooms, among them, Grace Lumpkin, Willie Gropper the cartoonist, Helen O'Lochlain Crowe, Michael Gold, a man or two whose names I never knew — yet I recall that one of them said, "Damn it, I'm through. I'd like to leave this country!" Someone asked bitterly, "Well, where would you go?" and half a dozen voices called as one, "Russia!" in their infatuated ignorance, but it was touching because of its sincerity; there was a fervor like an old-fashioned American revival meeting in them and there was a bond between them. Some of them were the children of the oldest governing families and founders of this nation, and an astonishing number were children of country preachers or teachers or doctors — the "salt of the earth" — besides the first-born generation of emigrants who had braved the escape, the steerages, the awful exile, to reach this land where the streets, they had heard, were paved with gold. I felt somewhat alien from this company because of my experience with would-be Communists in Mexico and because of my recent exposure to the view of a genuine Party official; yet in those days, I was still illusioned to the extent that I half accepted the entirely immoral doctrine that one *should* go along with the Devil if he worked on your side; but my few days in the same office with Rosa Baron and her crowd had shaken this theory too, as it proved, to the foundation. Two truisms: The end does *not* justify the means and one I discovered for myself then and there, The Devil is *never* on your side except for his own purposes.

Does all of this sound very old-fashioned, like the Communist vocabulary or the early Freudian theories? Well, it was fifty years ago and I am not trying to bring anything up-to-date. I am trying to sink back into the past and recreate a certain series of events recorded in scraps at the time which have haunted me painfully for life.

Somebody suggested that he would like a drink. Michael Gold said he knew where to find it and went out and bought a bottle of bootleg gin; and then, nobody wanted to drink after all except one girl I have not named — an Irish Catholic girl I had never known to be anything but tender and gentle, now strode up and down the room in pure hysteria, swinging the open bottle of gin and singing in a loud flat voice a comic old song about an Irish wake: "They took the ice from off the corpse and put it in the beer — your feyther was a grand old man — give us a drink!" and she would upend the bottle and take a swig with a terrible tragic face and try to hand it around. Somebody shouted the first line of the Internationale; someone else began *"Giovinezza, giovinezza! Primavera di bellezza!"* drowning each other out and the hysterical striding girl too — I was ashamed of it, for it was no moment for a low sense of humor to assert itself, or so it seemed to me, but I thought, "Suppose I started singing 'The Star-Spangled Banner'? I bet I'd get thrown out of a window!" I felt a chill of distrust or estrangement — I was far from home, a stranger in a strange land indeed, for the first time in my life.

"No, don't, darling," said one of the men to the girl as she went on crying her tuneless chorus aloud, pouring the raw gin down her throat as she changed her tune to the gibberish of "The Battle Hymn of the Republic." "In the beauty of the lilies, Christ was born across the sea," she sang the silly words to the claptrap tune in march time, striding back and forth. The Communist sympathizers and the Jews alike flinched, offended, and all the faces turned sour, frowning.

"Jesus," said Mike Gold, "leave Christ out of this!"

"With a glory in His bosom that transfigures you and me," sang the girl, swinging the bottle and marching, her eyes blinded, her face as white as a frosted lantern.

"We've got to *stop* her," said a young woman — I don't remember who, but I remember the words — "This is dangerous!" and she must have heard them too, for she turned instantly and broke from the room and ran down the hall toward the window at the end. Several of us ran after her and two of the men seized her from the open window. She broke into submissive tears and gave way at once. They brought her back and we put her to bed, fully dressed, then and there; she slept almost at once. The rest of us sat up nearly all night, with nothing to say, nothing to do, brought to a blank pause, keeping a vigil with the dead in the first lonely long night of death. It was no consolation to say their long ordeal was ended. It was not ended for us — and perhaps I should speak for myself — their memory was already turning to stone in my mind. In my whole life I have never felt such a weight of pure bitterness, helpless anger in utter defeat, outraged love and hope, as hung over us all in that room — or did we breathe it out of ourselves? A darkness of shame, too, settled down with us, a most deplorable kind of shame. It was in every pair of eyes that met other eyes in furtive roving. Shame at our useless, now self-indulgent emotions, our disarmed state, our absurd lack of spirit. At last we broke up and parted —

I remember nothing more of this incident. It dissolves and disappears like salt poured into water — but the salt taste is there.

In the morning when we began straggling out in small parties on our way to the trial, several of us went down in the elevator with three entirely correct old gentlemen looking much alike in their sleekness, pinkness, baldness, glossiness of grooming, such stereotypes as no proletarian novelist of the time would have dared to use as the example of a capitalist monster in his novel. We were pale and tight-faced; our eyelids were swollen; no doubt in spite of hot coffee and cold baths, we looked rumpled, unkempt, disreputable, discredited, vaguely guilty, pretty well frayed out by then. The gentlemen regarded us glossily, then turned to each other. As we descended the many floors in silence, one of them said to the others in a cream-cheese voice, "It is very pleasant to know we may expect things to settle down properly again," and the others nodded with wise, smug, complacent faces.

To this day, I can feel again my violent desire just to slap his whole slick face all over at once, hard, with the flat of my hand, or better, some kind of washing bat or any useful domestic appliance being applied where it would really make an impression — a butter paddle — something he would feel through that smug layer of too-well-fed fat. For a long time after, I felt that I had sprained my very soul in the effort I had to make resisting that impulse to let fly.

I shut my eyes and clenched my hands behind me
and saw, in lightning flashes, myself doing ferocious
things, like pushing him down an endless flight of
stairs, or dropping him without warning into a bot-
tomless well, or stringing him up to a stout beam and
leaving him to dangle, or — or other things of the
sort; no guns, no knives, no baseball bats, nothing to
cause outright bloodshed, just silent, grim, sudden
murder by hand was my intention. All this was far
beyond my bodily powers of course, and I like to believe beyond my criminal powers too. For I woke
when we struck the searing hot light of the August
morning as if I had come out of a nightmare, horri-
fied at my own thoughts and feeling as if I had got
some incurable wound to my very humanity — as
indeed I had. However inflicted, a wound there was,
with painful scar tissue, left upon my living self by
that appalling event. My conscience stirs as if, in my
impulse to do violence to my enemy, I had assisted at
his crime.

In the huge, bare, dusty room where the court sat, it
was instantly clear that the Pink Tea Squad had been
taken off duty for this round. We were all huddled
in together — I don't remember any chairs — and
stood around, or sat on the grimy floor or on a shal-
low flight of steps leading I forget where; the place
was as dismal and breathless as a tenement fire escape in August. Big, overmuscled, beefy policemen

with real thug faces bawled at us senselessly (we were all of us merely passive by then), crowded in among us to keep us moving and generally hustled us around, not violently, just viciously and sordidly and impudently, by way of showing what they *could* do if sufficiently provoked. We were forbidden to smoke but I tried it anyway — the whole scene struck me as just second-rate melodrama, nothing to be taken seriously anymore. John Dos Passos, sitting near me, held a spread newspaper above me while I snatched a whiff, but we were seen and yelled at. I was sorry then to have involved him in such a useless disturbance, though he did not seem in the least to mind; he always had in those days — I have hardly seen him since[4] — a wonderful, gentle composure of manner, and I have never forgotten his expression of amiable distance from the whole grubby scene as I put out the cigarette and he folded his newspaper, while the greasy, sweating man in the blue suit stood above us and went on glaring and bawling a little longer, just in case we had not heard him the first time.

Mrs. Stuart Chase, who had been faithfully on the picket line and was now waiting trial with the rest, also had been one of the speakers at some of the rallies; she showed me several anonymous letters she had received, of an unbelievable obscenity and threatening her with some very imaginative mutila-

---

[4] He died long after this was written.

tions. It was Mrs. Chase who told me that there was a rumor afloat that we were going to be treated simply as common nuisances, the charge was to be "loitering and obstructing traffic"! Arthur Garfield Hayes, the attorney for all of us, for all the various defense committees, had explained that if we were to be tried on the real charge, God knew where it would end, there could easily be embarrassing consequences all around — more to the prosecution than to us, it seemed, and I remember wondering why, at that point, we should be troubled to spare their feelings. Naturally it turned out not to be a matter of feelings in any direction but of legal points obscure to perhaps any but the legal mind. There was then in existence — is it still, I wonder? — an infamous law called Baumes' Law, which provided that anyone who had been arrested as much as four times — or was it *more* than four times? — should be eligible to imprisonment for life. There were a good number of perennial, roving, year-round emergency picketers in that group — people whose good pleasure it was to join almost any picket line on sight, and of course they would be arrested sooner or later and these arrests could mount up to a pretty respectable number very soon. One woman said to me, "Suppose I told them I've been arrested seventeen times?" and I said, "Well, why *don't* you?" but of course she could not because for one thing she was not allowed to get within speaking distance of the court.

However, on getting this news straight, about

twenty-five of us decided that under Baumes' Law (some of us couldn't believe such a monstrosity existed on our statute books; we thought someone was playing a low joke on our ignorance) we must surely be more than eligible for at least ninety-nine years each in the clink and decided to agitate for it. Our plan was to make a point of forcing them to observe that lunatic Baumes' Law and overload their jails. For a number of us, writers and artists of all kinds particularly, it might so nicely have settled the problem of where we were to eat and sleep while writing that book or doing whatever it was we had in mind. In those days it was believed that political prisoners were not treated too badly; we learned our mistake later, that it was the big gangsters who were treated well, but at that time, in our innocence, it looked to some of us like the last broad highway to the practice of the arts.

It was not to be; we should have known from the first. The prisoners who had records of more than three arrests were simply pushed back into a captive audience, while several celebrities from various walks were chosen as tokens to stand trial for all of us. I remember of them — a half-dozen — only Edna St. Vincent Millay and Paxton Hibben. It was worth going there to see our attorney, Arthur Garfield Hayes, in confidential palaver with the judge, a little old gray man with pointed whiskers and the face of a smart, conspiratorial chipmunk. In a single rolling sentence the judge, not just with a straight face but portentously, as if pronouncing another death sentence, found us guilty of loitering and obstructing traffic, fined us five dollars each, and the tragic farce took its place in history.

When two or three of our number tried to raise and demand separate trials on sterner grounds, they were squelched by everybody — the judge, our attorney, the policemen, and even their own neighbors — for a lot of them were after all home-keeping persons who had come out, as you might say, on borrowed time and now were anxious to get back home again. The judge, the lawyers, the police, the whole court, the whole city of Boston, and the State of Massachusetts desired nothing in the world so much as to be rid of us, to see the last of us forever, to hear the last of this scandal (though they have never, alas, and will never!), and all the slightest signs of dissent from any direction were so adroitly and quickly suppressed that even the most enthusiastic troublemaker never quite knew how it was done. Simply our representatives were tried in a group in about five minutes.

A busy, abstracted woman wearing pinch-nose spectacles, whom I never saw before or since, pushed her way among us, pressing five dollars into every hand, instructing us one and all to pay our fines, then and there, which we did. I do not in the least remember how my note changed hands again, but no doubt I gave it to the right person as all of us did, and there we were, out on the sidewalk again, discredited once for all, it seemed, mere vagrants but in movement, no longer loitering and obstructing traffic. "Get on there," yelled our policemen, "get going there, keep moving"; and their parting advice to us was that we all go back where we came from and stay there. It was their next-best repartee, but a poor, thin substitute for one good whack at our skulls with their truncheons.

I returned to the hotel and found the temporary office already being dismantled. Another woman came up and said, "Are you packed and ready to go?" She pressed into my hand a railroad ticket to New York and ten dollars in cash. "Go straight to the station now and take the next train," she said. I did this with no farewells and no looking back. I found several other persons, some of whom I had sat up with nearly all night more than once, also being banished from the scene of the crime. We greeted each other without surprise or pleasure and scattered out singly and separately with no desire for each other's company. I do not even remember who many of them were, if I ever knew their names at all. I only remember our silence and the dazed melancholy in all the faces.

In all this I should speak only for myself, for never in my life have I felt so isolated as I did in that host of people, all presumably moved in the same impulse, with the same or at least sympathetic motive;

when one might think hearts would have opened, minds would respond with kindness we did not find it so, but precisely the contrary. I went through the time in a mist of unbelief, or the kind of unwillingness to believe what is passing before one's eyes that comes often in nightmares. But before in my sleep I could always say, "It is only a dream and you will wake and wonder at yourself for being frightened." But I was suffering, I know it now, from pure fright, from shock — I was not an inexperienced girl, I was thirty-seven years old; I knew a good deal about the evils and abuses and cruelties of the world; I had known victims of injustice, of crime. I was not ignorant of history, nor of literature; I had witnessed a revolution in Mexico, had in a way taken part in it, had seen it follow the classic trail of all revolutions. Besides all the moral force and irreproachable motives of so many, I knew the deviousness and wickedness of both sides, on all sides, and the mixed motives — plain love of making mischief, love of irresponsible power, unscrupulous ambition of many men who never stopped short of murder, if murder would advance their careers an inch. But this was something very different, unfamiliar.

Now, through all this distance of time, I remember most vividly Mrs. Harriman's horsehair lace and flower garden party hats; Lola Ridge standing in the half darkness before Charlestown Prison under the rearing horse's hoofs; the gentle young girl striding and drinking gin from the bottle and singing her wake-dirges; Luigia Vanzetti's face as she stared in horror down into the crowd howling like beasts; and Rosa Baron's little pinpoints of eyes glittering through her spectacles at me and her shrill, accusing voice: "Saved? Who wants them saved? What earthly good would they do us alive?"

I CANNOT even now decide by my own evidence whether or not they were guilty of the crime for which they were put to death. They expressed in their letters many thoughts, if not always noble, at least elevated, exalted even. Their fervor and human feelings gave the glow of life to the weary stock phrases of those writing about them, and we do know now, all of us, that the most appalling cruelties are committed by apparently virtuous governments in expectation of a great good to come, never learning that the evil done now is the sure destroyer of the expected good. Yet, no matter what, it was a terrible miscarriage of justice; it was a most reprehensible abuse of legal power, in their attempt to prove that the law is something to be inflicted — not enforced — and that it is above the judgment of the people.

AFTERWORD

I HAVE, for my own reasons, refused to read any book or any article on the Sacco–Vanzetti trial before I had revised or arranged my notes on this trial. Since I have finished, I have read the book by Herbert B. Ehrmann, the "last surviving lawyer involved in the substance of the case on either side," who, I feel, tells the full story of the case. Also, I have read since I finished my story "The Never-Ending Wrong," the article by Francis Russell in the *National Review*, page 887 of August 17, 1973, which was discovered among my magazines early last year and which I have decided should be the epigraph to this story. Mr. Russell believes that the fact that Dante Sacco, Nicola Sacco's son, kept his superhuman or subhuman silence on the whole history of his father proves that Nicola Sacco was guilty; that he refused to confess and so implicated Vanzetti, who died innocent. Sacco, therefore, proved himself doubly, triply, a murderer, an instinctive killer. Maybe.

Another maybe — Vanzetti's speech at the electric chair was the final word of an honest man. It is proven by testimony that he was innocent of murder. He was selling eels on that day, for Christmas. The Italian tradition of eating eels on Christmas Eve occupied his time all that day. He called on all the families he knew who were his friends, to deliver their orders for eels, and during the trial these people, when questioned, told exactly the same story, even to each housewife remembering the hour he delivered the eels, and some of them even went so far as to say how they had prepared them. Their testimonies were ignored when the real trial was begun. Mr. Russell has, I think, overlooked one point in his argument. Vanzetti was comrade-in-arms and in mind and heart with Sacco. They were Anarchists foresworn, committed for life to death, for death was the known fate of all who were brought to trial for the crime, as it was considered. My point is this: Sacco was guilty if you like; some minor points make it reasonable, though *barely* reasonable, to believe it. Vanzetti knew his will and he believed in the cause which he knew contained death for him unless he was very lucky indeed. Anarchy is a strange belief to die for, but my good friend in Mexico, Felipe Carillo, the Governor of Yucatan, explained to me why the revolutionists in his country who were robbing trains, wrecking haciendas, burning houses, destroying crops and even whole villages of helpless people, were right. In their utter misery, they gathered money with violence, seized the materials built with their blood, to create their idea of a good society. It was right to destroy material evil and to take its loot for their cause.

This is the doctrine of desperation, the last murderous rage before utter despair. They were wrong, but not more wrong than the thing they themselves were trying to destroy. The powerful society they opposed gained its power and grew up on the same methods they were taking. Vanzetti kept a sacred pact, not just with his comrade Sacco but with the whole great solemn oath of his life, to the cause of freedom. He fasted, kept his silence, and went to his death with his fellow, a sacrifice to his faith. As he was being strapped into the electric chair, he said, "I wish to tell you that I am an innocent man. I never committed any crime but sometimes some sin. I wish to forgive *some* people for what they are now doing to me." They both spoke nobly at the end, they kept faith with their vows for each other. They left a great heritage of love, devotion, faith, and courage — all done with the sure intention that holy Anarchy should be glorified through their sacrifice and that the time would come that no human being should be humiliated or be made abject. Near the end of their ordeal Vanzetti said that if it had not been for "these thing" he might have lived out his life talking at street corners to scorning men. He might have died unmarked, unknown, a failure. "Now, we are not a failure. This is our career and our triumph. Never in our full life could we hope to do such work for tolerance, for justice, for man's understanding of man as now we do by accident. Our words — our lives — our pains — nothing! The taking of our lives — lives of a good shoemaker and a poor fish peddler — all!

That last moment belongs to us — that agony is our triumph."

This is not new — all the history of our world is pocked with it. It is very grand and noble in words and grand, noble souls have died for it — it is worth weeping for. But it doesn't work out so well. In order to annihilate the criminal State, they have become criminals. The State goes on without end in one form or another, built securely on the base of destruction. Nietzsche said: "The State is the coldest of all cold monsters," and the revolutions which destroy or weaken at least one monster bring to birth and growth another.

FAR away and long ago, I read Emma Goldman's story of her life, her first book in which she told the grim, deeply touching narrative of her young life during which she worked in a scrubby sweatshop making corsets by the bundle. At the same time, I was reading Prince Kropotkin's memoirs, his account of the long step he took from his early princely living to his membership in the union of the outcast, the poor, the depressed, and it was a most marvelous thing to have two splendid, courageous, really noble human beings speaking together, telling the same tale. It was like a duet of two great voices telling a tragic story. I believed in both of them at once. The two of them joined together left me no answerable argument; their dream was a grand one but it was exactly that — a dream. They both lived to know this and I learned it from them, but it has not changed my love for them or my lifelong sympathy for the cause to which they devoted their lives — to ameliorate the anguish that human beings inflict on each other — the never-ending wrong, forever incurable.

In 1935 in Paris, living in that thin upper surface of comfort and joy and freedom in a limited way, I met this most touching and interesting person, Emma Goldman, sitting at a table reserved for her at the Select, where she could receive her friends and carry on her conversations and sociabilities over an occasional refreshing drink. She was half blind (although she was only sixty-six years old), wore heavy spectacles, a shawl, and carpet slippers. She lived in her past and her devotions, which seemed to her glorious and unarguably right in every purpose. She accepted the failure of that great dream as a matter of course. She finally came to admit sadly that the human race in its weakness demanded government and all government was evil because human nature was basically weak and weakness is evil. She was a wise, sweet old thing, grandmotherly, or like a great-aunt. I said to her, "It's a pity you had to spend your whole life in such unhappiness when you could have had such a nice life in a good government, with a home and children."

She turned on me and said severely: "What have

I just said? There is no such thing as a good government. There never was. There can't be."

I closed my eyes and watched Nietzsche's skull nodding.

This list of books has been prepared from among those I read about cases that will not end . . .

1. Haim Cohen, *The Trial and Death of Jesus.* New York: Harper and Row, 1963.

2. *The Trial of Joan of Arc* (The verbatim report of the proceedings from the Orléans Manuscript, translated with an introduction and notes by W. S. Scott). London: The Folio Society, 1971.

3. Régine Pernoud, *Joan of Arc.* New York: Evergreen Press, 1961.

4. *Report of Court Proceedings in the Case of The Anti-Soviet Trotskyite Center.* The People's Commissariat of Justice of the USSR, Moscow, 1937.

5. *The Letters of Sacco and Vanzetti,* edited by Marion D. Frankfurter and Gardner Jackson. New York: Viking Press, 1928.

6. Herbert B. Ehrmann, *The Case That Will Not Die.* Boston: Little, Brown and Company, 1969.